D1101958

The Swoose

Dick King-Smith served in the Grenadier Guards during the Second World War, and afterwards spent twenty years as a farmer in Gloucestershire, the county of his birth. Many of his stories are inspired by his farming experiences. Later he taught at a village primary school. His first book, *The Fox Busters*, was published in 1978. Since then he has written a great number of children's books, including *The Sheep-Pig* (winner of the Guardian Award and filmed as *Babe*), *Harry's Mad*, *Noah's Brother*, *The Hodgeheg*, *Martin's Mice*, *Ace*, *The Cuckoo Child* and *Harriet's Hare* (winner of the Children's Book Award in 1995). At the British Book Awards in 1991 he was voted Children's Author of the Year. He has three children, a large number of grandchildren and several great-grandchildren, and lives in a seventeenth-century cottage only a crow's flight from the house where he was born.

Dick King-Smith
The Swoose

Illustrated by Ann Kronheimer

PUFFIN

PUFFIN BOOKS

Published by the Penguin Group
Penguin Books Ltd, 80 Strand, London WC2R 0RL, England
Penguin Group (USA), Inc., 375 Hudson Street, New York, New York 10014, USA
Penguin Books Australia Ltd, 250 Camberwell Road, Camberwell, Victoria 3124, Australia
Penguin Books Canada Ltd, 10 Alcorn Avenue, Toronto, Ontario, Canada M4V 3B2
Penguin Books India (P) Ltd, 11 Community Centre, Panchsheel Park, New Delhi – 110 017, India
Penguin Group (NZ), cnr Airborne and Rosedale Roads, Albany, Auckland 1310, New Zealand
Penguin Books (South Africa) (Pty) Ltd, 24 Sturdee Avenue, Rosebank 2196, South Africa

Penguin Books Ltd, Registered Offices: 80 Strand, London WC2R 0RL, England

www.penguin.com

First published by Viking 1993
Published in Puffin Books 1994
Published in this edition 2005
5

Text copyright © Fox Busters Ltd, 1993
Illustrations copyright © Ann Kronheimer, 2005
All rights reserved

The moral right of the author and illustrator has been asserted

Set in 17/22.25pt Perpetua

Made and printed in England by Clays Ltd, St Ives plc

Except in the United States of America, this book is sold subject to the condition that it shall not, by
way of trade or otherwise, be lent, re-sold, hired out, or otherwise circulated without the publisher's
prior consent in any form of binding or cover other than that in which it is published and without a
similar condition including this condition being imposed on the subsequent purchaser

British Library Cataloguing in Publication Data
A CIP catalogue record for this book is available from the British Library

ISBN-13: 978-0-14-131824-0

www.greenpenguin.co.uk

Mixed Sources
Product group from well-managed
forests and other controlled sources
www.fsc.org Cert no. SA-COC-1592
© 1996 Forest Stewardship Council

Penguin Books is committed to a sustainable future
for our business, our readers and our planet.
The book in your hands is made from paper
certified by the Forest Stewardship Council.

One

'Mum,' said Fitzherbert. 'Why do I look different from all the other goslings on the farm?'

He did, there was no denying it. He was larger than the rest, his feet were bigger, and his neck was longer.

'You *are* different,' said his mother.

'Because I'm an only child, d'you mean?'

The other geese all had five or six goslings apiece, but Fitzherbert alone had hatched from his mother's clutch of eggs.

'An only child in more ways than one,' she said. 'I doubt if there's another bird like you in the whole wide world. All these other youngsters will grow up to be ordinary common or garden geese, but not you, Fitzherbert my boy.'

'But I'm a goose like you, Mum, aren't I?' said Fitzherbert.

'No,' said his mother, 'you are not.'

She lowered her voice.

'You,' she said softly, 'are a swoose.'

Fitzherbert coiled his long neck backwards into the shape of an S.

'A what?' he cried.

'Sssssssh!' hissed his mother, and she waddled off to a distant corner of the farmyard, away from all the other geese.

Fitzherbert hurried after her.

'What did you say I was?' he asked.

His mother looked around to make sure they were out of earshot of the rest of the flock, and then she said, 'Now listen carefully. What I am about to tell you must be a secret between you and

me, always. D'you understand?'

'Yes, Mum,' said Fitzherbert.

'You are old enough now to be told,' said his mother, 'why you are unlike all the other goslings on the farm. They are the children of a number of geese, but all of them have the same father.'

'The old grey gander, you mean?'

'Yes.'

'But isn't he my father too?'

'No.'

'Then who is?'

'Your father,' said Fitzherbert's mum, and a dreamy look came over her face as she spoke, 'is neither old nor grey. Your father is young and strong and as white as the driven snow. Never shall I forget the day we met!'

'Where was that, Mum?'

'It was by the river. I had gone down by myself for a swim, when suddenly he appeared, high in the sky above. Oh, the music of his great wings! It was love at first flight! Then he landed on the surface in a shower of spray and swam towards me.'

'But I don't get it, Mum,' said

Fitzherbert. 'What was he? Another sort of goose?'

'No,' said his mother. 'He was a swan.'

'What's that?'

'A swan is the most beautiful of all birds, and your father was the most beautiful of all swans.'

'What was his name?'

'He didn't say. He was a mute swan.'

Fitzherbert thought about all this for a while.

Then he said, 'So I might be the only swoose in the world?'

'Yes.'

'There aren't any other swooses?'

'Sweese.'

'Eh?'

'When there's more than one goose, you say geese. So more than one swoose would be sweese.'

'But there isn't more than one. Just

me. You just said so, didn't you?'

As mothers do, Fitzherbert's mum became fed up with his constant questions.

'Oh, run away and play,' she said.

But playing with the other goslings wasn't a lot of fun for Fitzherbert. Already they had noticed that he was different. They poked fun at him, calling him Bigfeet or Snakyneck, and they wouldn't let him join in their games.

Time passed, and Fitzherbert began to grow his adult feathers. Often, as he thought of his father swooping down from the sky on whistling wings, he flapped his own and wished that he too could fly. Farmyard geese like his mother

and the rest couldn't, he knew – they were too heavy-bodied to get off the ground. But swans could. How about a swoose? And the more he thought about his father, the more he wanted to meet him. So one day he decided to go down to the river by himself. He would say nothing to his mother about it, but just set off when she wasn't looking.

He had never before been out of the farmyard, and he was not at all sure

what the river looked like, let alone where it was, but luck was on his side. He walked across a couple of fields and there it was, in front of him!

Fitzherbert looked at the wide stretch of water, winking and gleaming in the sunlight and chuckling to itself as it flowed along. Never in his life had he swum upon anything but the duckpond at the farm, but this – this is the place for swimming, he thought, and he

waddled down the bank and pushed off.

He paddled about in midstream, looking up at the sky, hoping that a snow-white shape would come gliding down to greet him.

Instead he suddenly turned to see a whole armada of snow-white shapes sailing silently downstream towards him. There must have been at least twenty swans, all making for this stranger who dared to swim upon their river. Their wings were curved in excitement, and the look in their black eyes was far from friendly.

Oh, thought Fitzherbert, as the fleet of swans approached, all now grunting and hissing angrily, oh dear, I really must fly!

Two

As Fitzherbert swam hastily away from
his pursuers, he spread his wings and beat
them madly on the water in an effort to
increase his speed. Harder and harder he
flapped, and then he felt his body lift a
little so that now, instead of swimming,
he was slapping his broad webs on the
surface in a kind of clumsy run.

Suddenly he was airborne, and the swans, satisfied that they had seen off the stranger, did not trouble to follow.

It wasn't much of a flight, that first effort. For perhaps a quarter of a mile, Fitzherbert laboured along only a few yards above the water, and then, tired out by his efforts, flopped back down into the river. He looked anxiously around, but to his great relief, there was no sign of the swans. Nasty, bad-tempered creatures, he said to himself. I wasn't doing them any harm. Why, my dad might have been one of that lot. I don't know that I want to meet him after all.

He swam on, looking about him with interest. He could see other birds on the

water – different sorts of duck, and
moorhen, and coot – and there was a
sudden brilliant flash of colour as a king-
fisher darted across. There were people
on the river too, in rowing boats and
punts, and one very long thin craft shot
by with eight large young men pulling at
their oars, while a ninth much smaller
man steered and shouted at them
through a kind of tube held to his mouth.

'In! Out! In! Out!' he called, and the blades dipped and rose as one.

Fitzherbert drifted dreamily with the current, enjoying the sunlit scene, when suddenly a sharp voice cried, 'Avast there, you landlubber, or you'll run us down!'

Startled, the swoose looked down to meet the angry gaze of a small water vole.

'Oh, sorry!' said Fitzherbert. 'I'm afraid I wasn't looking where I was going.'

The vole did not answer, but swam to the bank. Fitzherbert followed.

'I suppose you couldn't tell me?' he said.

The vole turned at the mouth of his burrow.

'Tell you what?' he said.

'Where I'm going?'

The vole stared beadily at the swoose.

'Are you feather-brained?' he said.

'No, I'm Fitzherbert.'

The water vole shook his blunt head as
though to clear it.

'Tell us something,' he said. 'You come
sailing along without any regard for the
rule of the river, and then you go and

talk a load of rubbish. Anyways, I never
in my life set eyes on a bird like you
before. What are you?'

'I'm a . . .' began Fitzherbert, and then
he thought, oh no, I promised Mum I
wouldn't tell.

'I can't really say,' he replied.

'You don't know what you are,' said
the vole. 'You don't know where you're

going. Next thing, you'll be telling me you don't know what river this is.'

'No. I don't.'

'Then you don't know the name of that town you can see, down at the end of the reach?'

'No.'

'Nor the castle on the hill above it?'

'No.'

'Nor who lives in that castle?'

'No,' said Fitzherbert. 'I've never been outside our farmyard before. But I'd be very grateful if you'd tell me.'

'You're lucky, young fellow,' said the vole. 'You've come to the right chap. Now, if you'd asked a moorhen, or worse, a duck, you'd have been wasting your breath. But there isn't much that I

don't know about this here stretch of the
Thames.'

'The what?'

'The Thames. That's the name of this
river. Most famous river in all England,
I'd say. And that town yonder is Windsor,
and that's Windsor Castle above it. Now
then, surely you know who lives there?'

'No.'

'Why, the Queen, of course.'

'Oh,' said Fitzherbert. 'What's a queen?' he said.

The water vole sighed deeply.

'You're a bright one,' he said. 'She's only the most important person in the land, that's all.'

At this point a pair of swans appeared in midstream.

Fitzherbert backed into a clump of reeds and kept his head down.

'Now d'you see those swans?' said the vole. 'They belong to the Queen, they do, like every other swan in the country. Royal birds, swans are.'

Oh, thought Fitzherbert, I wonder if sweese are? I bet she's never seen one.

'This queen,' he said. 'What's she called?'

'Victoria. She's been Queen for donkey's years, she has.'

'Donkey's ears?' said Fitzherbert.

'Why, 'tis ages ago she lost her husband.'

'Couldn't she find him again?'

The water vole sighed and continued.

'And ever since she's shut herself up in that castle. Always dressed in black, she is. The Widow of Windsor, they call her.'

'How do you know all these things?' asked Fitzherbert.

'I keep my ears open,' said the water vole. 'Windsor folk come out boating on the river and I listen to all the latest gossip.'

'She doesn't sound very happy, this queen,' said Fitzherbert.

'She isn't. Grumpy old thing, from all accounts.'

'Perhaps she needs cheering up.'

'Easier said than done. Anybody tries making a joke, she says, "We are not amused",' said the vole, and with that he vanished into his burrow.

A moment later he stuck his head out
again.

'She might be amused at you,' he said.
'Why don't you pay her a visit?'

Why don't I? thought the swoose.

'I will,' he said, 'and I'll come back
and tell you all about it.'

Then it occurred to him that there
were probably a great many water voles
living beside the Thames.

'So can you tell me your name,
please?' he said.

'Alph,' said the vole, and he disappeared
once more.

Three

Dressed all in black, Queen Victoria stood at an upper window in Windsor Castle and looked down at the courtyard below. In the centre of this courtyard was a perfect square of brilliantly green grass, a lawn that was not only personally mown by the Royal Head Gardener, but afterwards finely manicured by a number of under-gardeners. No other feet were allowed upon this lawn, save those of the Queen's pet dogs and of the footman who tidied up after them with an elegant brass shovel.

But now it seemed there was a large shape, right in the centre of the square of green.

The Queen held out a hand.

'Our pince-nez,' she said to her Lady of the Bedchamber, and when these were brought, she fitted them upon the bridge of the Royal nose.

For some moments she stared down, and then she said, 'And what, pray, is that?'

'It is a bird, ma'am,' said the Lady of the Bedchamber.

'We can see that,' said Queen Victoria.
'We are not blind. See that it is removed
immediately. Whatever is it doing on our
grass?' and she turned away from the
window.

The Lady of the Bedchamber heaved a
sigh of relief that she'd avoided having to
answer the Queen's last question. She

could see plainly what the bird had that moment done on the grass.

'That's better!' said Fitzherbert as he waddled away from the large squelchy mess he had just made.

He was feeling pretty pleased with himself. Everything had gone swimmingly. He had swum on down the Thames, keeping well away from swans, and stopping every now and then to feed on juicy water-plants. It was late in the day before he came to the town, so he decided to

wait till next morning before visiting the castle.

At dawn Fitzherbert looked up to see its looming walls and towers. Good job sweese can fly, he thought, and he took off and flew up the hill.

The town of Windsor was still asleep and its streets were as yet empty of the busy horse-drawn traffic. Only a milkman driving his cart with its load of brass-bound wooden churns noticed a large bird fly up Castle Hill and over the

turrets of the Henry VIII Gate.

This, Fitzherbert's second flight, was altogether a much more successful effort. Even so, he tired rapidly, and, seeing a square of grass in an inner courtyard, he landed thankfully upon it. It was a crash-landing that knocked the wind out of him, and for some time he lay and gasped for breath.

Finally recovered, he looked about him. Then he saw a movement at an upper window. Someone was looking down at him. He could not see the figure clearly, but it appeared to be dressed in black!

If that's the Queen, thought Fitzherbert, I'd better make myself comfortable before I meet her. He stood up and

suited his actions to his words.

'That's better!' he said, and he waddled
off slowly towards the nearest door.
The Lady of the Bedchamber lost no
time in contacting the Lord Steward of
Her Majesty's Household.

'There's a large bird,' she said to him,
'in the Queen's private courtyard, and
she wants it removed immediately.'

'What sort of a bird?' asked the Lord
Steward.

'I don't know,' said the Lady of the Bedchamber. 'It was something like a swan. But, then again, it was something like a goose.'

The Lord Steward of Her Majesty's Household sent for the Ornithologist Royal, the man who looked after the Queen's birds.

'There's a large bird,' he said, 'in Her Majesty's private courtyard. Get rid of it, will you?'

'What sort of a bird?' asked the Ornithologist Royal.

'Part swan, part goose, apparently.'

'Part swan, part goose!' murmured the Ornithologist Royal excitedly to himself as he hurried to do the Lord Steward's bidding. 'Could it be . . .?

Could it be?'

When the door into the courtyard opened, Fitzherbert was disappointed to see a man emerge. He seemed a nice man, however, for he produced some pieces of bread which he offered to the swoose. But no sooner had Fitzherbert begun to eat them than he was grabbed, his wings pinioned to his sides, and he was carried, kicking and struggling, away.

'It is! It is!' said the Ornithologist
Royal as he listened to his captive's cries
of protest, a blend of the grunting bark
of an angry swan and the cackling of an
outraged goose. He carried Fitzherbert
to the Royal Menagerie, where all manner
of creatures were housed, presented as
gifts to the Queen by visiting foreign
rulers.

'It is!' said the Ornithologist Royal
again as he feasted his eyes upon
Fitzherbert, now shut in a large cage. 'I
had heard tales of such a bird, but never
thought to see one! It is a swoose!'

'That bird,' said the Lord Steward of Her
Majesty's Household later. 'Have you
dealt with it?'

'Yes,' said the Ornithologist Royal.

'What was it?'

'It is a swoose!' said the Ornithologist Royal. 'A cross between a swan and a goose! A *rara avis* indeed! Her Majesty should be told.'

The Lord Steward of Her Majesty's Household remembered enough of his Latin to say to the Lady of the Bedchamber, 'It's a rare bird, the one that was in the Queen's courtyard. Called a swoose apparently. Her Majesty should be told.'

Nervously, for the Queen did not like to be told things, preferring that people should not speak until they were spoken to, the Lady of the Bedchamber approached her sovereign.

'Forgive me, Your Majesty,' she said, 'but that bird that you saw earlier this morning . . .'

'Well?' said the Queen, her face set in its usual grim mode.

'I am given to understand, ma'am, that it is a swoose.'

'A what?'

'A swoose, ma'am.'

To the great astonishment of the Lady of the Bedchamber, something that might almost have been called a small smile appeared on the Royal face. Never

in all the many years she had served at court had the Lady of the Bedchamber seen such a thing.

'A swoose,' said Queen Victoria. 'Why, surely that must be part swan, part goose!'

'Perhaps Your Majesty might care to see the creature?' said the Lady of the Bedchamber.

'We would,' said the Queen.

So it was that Fitzherbert, puzzled and angry at being shut in, saw the doors of the Royal Menagerie opened by a pair of

bewigged footmen and a procession enter.

Followed by the Lord Steward, the Ornithologist Royal and the Lady of the Bedchamber, and attended by the Lord Chamberlain, the Comptroller of Her Majesty's Household, the Master of the Horse and several Ladies-in-Waiting, came a short dumpy figure, dressed all in black.

For some time Queen Victoria stared

at Fitzherbert without speaking.
Naturally no one else spoke.

Then the Queen said, 'Are we right? Is
this bird indeed half-swan and half-
goose?'

'Your Majesty is perfectly correct,' said
the Ornithologist Royal.

'And it is a rarity?'

'Indeed, ma'am.'

'We do not like to see it so imprisoned.
Open the door of its cage.'

'But, ma'am . . .' began the

Ornithologist Royal, fearing that the bird might misbehave itself in some way, might even (dreadful thought) peck the Royal ankles.

'Do as we say,' snapped the Queen, 'and look sharp about it,' and the Ornithologist Royal looked very sharp indeed.

Fitzherbert could, of course, understand nothing of the medley of sounds
that the humans made. However, it was
clear to him that, thanks to the Queen,
he was to be a prisoner no longer, and
he thought that he should show his
gratitude.

With measured tread he walked out of
the cage and stood at attention before

the Queen. Then he slowly uncurled his long neck and laid his head upon the ground at the very feet of the monarch in a gesture that was the nearest he could come to a courtly bow.

To the amazement of the Lord Steward of Her Majesty's Household and the Ornithologist Royal and the Lady of the Bedchamber and the Lord Chamberlain and the Comptroller of Her Majesty's Household and the Master of the Horse and the Ladies-in-Waiting and the two bewigged footmen, none of whom recalled ever seeing such a sight before, Queen Victoria looked down at the swoose and smiled broadly.

'We are amused,' said the Widow of Windsor.

Four

The news that something had made the Queen smile for the first time in a quarter of a century, or, in other words, since the death of her husband, Prince Albert, spread like wildfire among the courtiers at Windsor Castle. Not only had she smiled once, but had continued to do so, and had even spoken quite pleasantly to

a number of people. More, she had exchanged her widow's cap of black for one of white lace, and all because of that swoose!

'It's all so beautifully timed,' the Lord Steward of Her Majesty's Household said to the Lady of the Bedchamber. 'Next year it's the Queen's Golden Jubilee as you know, when the whole kingdom will be celebrating her fifty years on the throne, and she will have to go about and show herself to the people. How pleased they will be to see her wearing a happy face again after all those years of gloom. The greatest care must be taken of that bird.'

Unfortunately, it wasn't.

The very next morning, the

Ornithologist Royal came in armed with a large pair of scissors. He intended to clip the flight feathers of one of the swoose's wings, a painless operation which would render the bird incapable of flight. Little did he guess that Fitzherbert had plans of his own.

First, despite having been released from his cage the previous evening on the Queen's orders, he had been shut up again as soon as she had gone, and this he did not like.

Second, he was longing to tell the water vole all about his audience with Queen Victoria.

So the moment the Ornithologist Royal opened the cage, Fitzherbert pushed past him and made his way as fast

as he could along a corridor and out
through a door.

'Stop! Stop!' cried the Ornithologist
Royal, hurrying after him, scissors in
hand, and then could only stand and
watch in horror as the swoose took wing
and flew away towards the Thames.

Fitzherbert flew upriver, trying to
remember whereabouts it was that he
had met the vole, when suddenly he saw
him swimming across a little backwater.

'Alph!' he cried, and swooping down, landed with a great splash. He looked around, but could only see a couple of moorhens that squawked angrily at him from the rushes.

Then he saw a blunt brown head break surface.

'Alph!' he cried again. 'Remember me?'

'How could I forget you?' said the vole sharply. 'First time we met, you nearly ran me down, and now you drop out of the sky almost on top of me. You're a clumsy great hummock and no mistake.'

'Sorry, Alph,' said Fitzherbert. 'I was in a hurry to tell you. I've seen the Queen! And what d'you think – she smiled at me!'

'Fancy!' said Alph.

He swam to the bank, and climbed out
and shook himself.

'Wonder why?' he said.

'I don't really know,' said Fitzherbert.
'She seemed to like me. And they were
all very pleased. Everyone was ever so
nice to me.'

'They didn't shut you up then?' said
Alph.

'Well, yes, they did, but I escaped.'

'What for?'

'Why, to come and find you and thank
you.'

'What for?'

'For suggesting I should visit the
Queen. It was a great idea. I must be
getting back now, I dare say Her
Majesty's missing me, wouldn't you
think?'

For a moment the water vole did not
answer. He sat on his haunches, combing
his very small round ears with his
forepaws. Then he fixed his very small
beady eyes on the swoose.

'I hope you know what you're doing,

young fellow,' he said. 'It's all very well
being the Queen's pet, but what if she
gets fed up with you, eh?'

'Well, then I suppose she'd just let me
go.'

'She might,' said Alph. 'Or she might
not. There's plenty of meat on you from

what I can see. You don't want to end up
like that, do you?'

'End up like what?' asked Fitzherbert.

'Eaten,' said Alph. 'At Windsor,' and
down his burrow he went.

Five

Meanwhile, back at the castle, panic reigned.

Everyone now knew that the swoose had flown away. Everyone, that is, except the Queen, and all were waiting, horrified, for the moment when she would find out.

The Ornithologist Royal in particular

was in a cold sweat. He had let the bird escape. He, everyone agreed, would lose his job.

So it was with a great sigh of relief that the worried man saw Fitzherbert come winging back over the battlements to

land once more in the inner courtyard. Armed with his scissors, he hurried out.

As he did so, an upper window was flung open and a commanding voice called out, 'Stop! And wait for us!'

The Ornithologist Royal stopped and waited, his heart in his mouth. What if the bird should take off again?

But Fitzherbert had no intention of doing so. To begin with, the flight to Alph and back had been quite tiring, and secondly, though he did not understand

the words, he recognized the note of command in the Royal tones.

In a little while Queen Victoria emerged from a side door into the courtyard, leaning upon the arm of the Lady of the Bedchamber.

The Ornithologist Royal was a tall man, but he felt very small at the sight of the dumpy little Queen's frowning face.

'What,' she said, 'are you doing with those scissors?'

'If you please,

Your Majesty,' said the Ornithologist Royal, 'I was intending to pinion the bird.'

'To pinion it?'

'To cut the flight feathers of one wing, ma'am.'

'With what object?'

'To prevent the bird from leaving you.'

'Leaving *us*?' said the Queen. 'Flying away, from *our* presence, do you mean? What an absurd idea! You will put those scissors away, sir, or it will be you who is leaving.'

Soon the whole court knew that, far from being chopped off, the feathers of the Queen's pet swoose must on no account be so much as ruffled. He was

to have the choicest food, such as fresh young vegetables from the kitchen gardens, brought to him by the Royal Head Gardener in person, and Scotch oatmeal porridge served by the Queen's manservant, John Brown.

In addition, the Royal Head Gardener's little daughter was appointed Swoosegirl-in-Waiting, to take Fitzherbert for daily walks in Windsor Great Park. By night, however, he was still shut in the Royal Menagerie for his own safety (for foxes, the Ornithologist Royal was sure, would be no respecters of sweese), but the Queen came in each evening to see her pet. Fitzherbert would make his bow, the Queen would smile, and everyone would heave a sigh

of relief at the welcome change that had
come over the crusty old lady.

At first Fitzherbert found the nights
trying. By day there were so many
people making a fuss of him, but at night
he was lonely. None of the other inmates
of the menagerie such as parrots or
monkeys bothered to talk to him, and he
thought how nice it would be to have a
chat with someone like Alph.

How pleasant it was then to hear a friendly voice one evening, just after the Queen and her company had left.

A cultured voice it was, a little singsong in tone, and altogether quite unlike the country voice of the water vole, though in fact it belonged to another rodent.

'How are you settling in, may one ask?' said the voice, and Fitzherbert looked up to see that the speaker was a rat.

He had come across rats before in the farmyard, ugly-looking creatures with rough brown coats, but this one was quite different.

To begin with, it was smaller and slenderer than a farm rat, with large thin ears and the longest of tails, longer even than its whole body. And second, that body was clothed in the glossiest of blue-black fur.

Altogether it was the most elegant animal, Fitzherbert thought, and he answered politely, 'Quite well, thank you.'

'Allow me to introduce myself,' said the black rat. 'My name is Maharanee.'

'Fitzherbert,' said the swoose.

'A noble-sounding name,' said Maharanee.

'So's yours,' said Fitzherbert. 'It sounds foreign.'

'So it is,' said the black rat. 'Her Majesty, as you may know, is also Empress of India, and her loyal subjects within the raj often send her gifts of animals. I stowed away with such a shipload, believing my proper place to be at court.'

'I don't quite understand,' said Fitzherbert.

'I myself am of Royal blood. I was

born in a palace, so it is fitting that I should associate myself with Her Majesty. Maharanee, you see, means "Great Queen".'

'Oh,' said Fitzherbert. 'So you're a favourite of hers too, are you?'

'I wouldn't exactly say that,' replied Maharanee. 'The English, you know, are less than friendly towards our brown

cousins and are apt to tar black rats with
the same brush. I tend therefore to keep
a low profile. But you certainly seem to
have taken Her Majesty's fancy. You're
quite the Royal pet.'

Until she gets fed up with me, thought
Fitzherbert, and then suddenly remembered that that was what Alph had said.

'Look here, Maharanee,' he said. 'You

don't suppose she'd ever . . . eat me, do you?'

The black rat looked at the swoose consideringly, and strangely, she too echoed Alph's words.

'She might,' she said. 'Or she might not. But if you are ever to be on the menu, I shall hear about it. I spend a good deal of time in the castle kitchens. Rely upon me to give you warning, Fitzherbert my friend.'

So the time passed pleasantly for the swoose. Not only did he enjoy the favour of the Queen, with all the benefits that came with it, but now he had two friends.

At night he had long and interesting

conversations with the much-travelled
Maharanee, and as often as he liked, he
flew upriver for a chat with the home-
spun Alph. To see the swoose go gave the
Ornithologist Royal
fifty fits at first, but
gradually he
became confident
that the bird would
always return.

All went well until the Head Cook and Bottlewasher at Windsor Castle reached retirement age and was replaced.

The black rat arrived in Fitzherbert's cage one evening in high excitement.

'What do you think!' she said. 'There is a French chef in the kitchen! No more stodgy, unimaginative English cooking. Now we shall see food fit for a Queen and leftovers fit for a Maharanee! There is nothing that a good chef cannot cook.'

Except sweese, I hope, thought Fitzherbert.

Six

Soon after this, some foreign cousins
of the Queen were due to stay at the
castle, and the new chef was instructed
to plan a modest ten-course dinner for
the visitors.

'And make sure that the main course
is something really spectacular, said the
Lord Steward.

The French chef sought the advice of the Queen's Butler.

'Is there something,' he asked, 'that only Royalty may eat, *monsieur*?'

The Queen's Butler thought for a moment.

'Why, yes,' he said. 'There is. Swan. Royal birds, swans are. No one else is allowed to eat them. There are plenty down there on the Thames.'

Roast swan and all the trimmings, thought the chef. That will indeed be *spectaculaire*!

All might yet have been well had not the chef lost his way in the many halls and corridors of the castle. One morning he took from his knife-rack the largest of his carving knives, closely watched,

though he did not know this, by an elegant
blue-black creature crouching beneath a
dresser.

He fingered the knife's edge, and then,
shaking his head at its bluntness, set off
to have it sharpened at the Armoury.
However, he failed to understand the
directions given him, and became con-
fused in the maze of passages.

Opening a door, he found himself in an

enclosed courtyard, in the centre of which was a perfect square of brilliantly green grass.

Right in the centre of it was a large shape.

The chef's hand tightened on his carving knife.

'*Voilà!*' he said softly. 'No need to go to the river. The bird has come to me!'

Fitzherbert was dozing, a little tired

after his daily walk. The Swoosegirl-in-Waiting had gone home to tea, and the Ornithologist Royal had not yet arrived to take the Queen's pet to the menagerie for the night.

Suddenly the swoose was woken by the voice of Maharanee.

'Fly, Fitzherbert, fly!' squealed the black rat.

Opening his eyes, the swoose saw a man approaching, a man dressed all in white and wearing a tall white hat, a man brandishing a huge knife!

At that very moment, a door opposite opened, and out of it, supported by her Lady of the Bedchamber, came Queen Victoria.

In his terror, Fitzherbert totally

disregarded Maharanee's instructions. Indeed, he completely forgot that he possessed his wild father's powers of flight and reverted to his mother's farmyard waddle.

Grunting, barking, cackling at the top of his voice, he hastened towards the Queen and turned and stood in front of her, his eyes fixed in horror on that dreadful knife that was destined, he was sure, for his throat.

Then, drawn by the terrible noise that the swoose was making, a host of people appeared and fell upon the wretched chef and dragged him away.

Later that evening, when all had been explained (and the luckless chef sent hurriedly back to France), the Queen came with her company into the menagerie. They brought a gilded chair for her, and she sat and looked at her swoose.

'What courage!' she said quietly. 'Not only did he sound the alarm, but he stood before us, thinking that we were to be murdered. He believed that he was saving us!'

Everyone looked at everyone else, but nobody said anything.

'We shall reward him for his bravery,'
said the Queen, and those nearest could
see that her old eyes were twinkling.

'Open the door of the cage,' she
commanded, and they opened it.

Fitzherbert stepped forward and stood
at attention before the monarch's chair,
and then, as always, lowered his head to
the floor.

The Queen looked round at her
courtiers and she positively grinned.

Then she raised her silver-headed,
ebony walking stick and with it she
lightly touched Fitzherbert upon one
shoulder.

'I dub thee Knight!' said Queen
Victoria in a loud voice. 'Arise, Sir
Swoose!'

And slowly, proudly, to a burst of
clapping from the smiling company of
watchers, Fitzherbert arose.